The King
and
the Magician

JORGE BUCAY

Illustrations by GUSTI

Abbeville Kids

AN IMPRINT OF ABBEVILLE PRESS

New York London

Once upon a time, in a faraway land, there lived a mighty King. He was so powerful, nothing could happen in the kingdom without his approval. It pleased the King to be so powerful, but that wasn't enough. The King commanded everyone in his realm to admire him as well as obey his every wish.

Each day the King would ask his subjects, "Who is the most powerful in the kingdom?" And out of fear, every day they answered: "You are the most powerful, Your Highness."

One day a rumor made its way to his Majesty's ears. Someone in his kingdom possessed a power that the King did not have.

In the village, there lived a humble Magician. The townspeople believed that the Magician had the ability to predict the future. The King feared that this ability would give the Magician even greater power than the King himself.

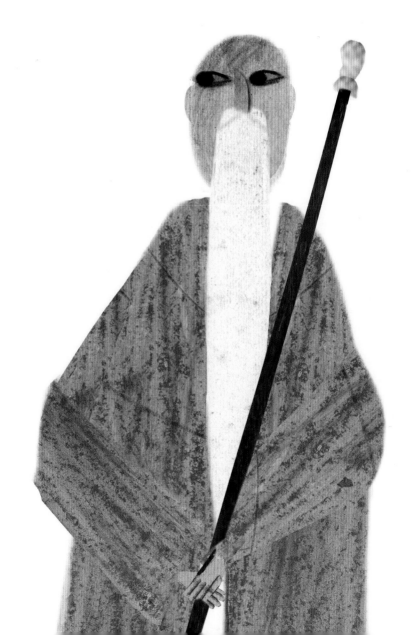

Alarmed, the King sent his soldiers and spies to investigate the rumors.

When his troops returned, they reported that not only could the Magician foresee the future, even worse, he was a wise and caring man, admired and loved by all.

This was unbearable for the King.
He became consumed by jealousy.

How could a ragged old man be
more powerful—and more loved—
than the strong and mighty King?

Full of hatred, he declared the
Magician his worst and most feared
enemy, and vowed to eliminate him.

The King devised an evil plan. He would host a grand party and invite this Magician to his palace. After the feast, he would demand everyone's attention and ask the Magician if it was true that he could tell the future.

If the Magician answered "No," it would be clear that he was only a simple trickster with no power at all.

If he answered "Yes," the King would ask him to prove his wizardry by predicting the day of the Magician's own death.

Whatever he answered, the King would take out his sword and kill him.

No one would ever again doubt that the King was the most powerful man in the land.

Pleased with his plot, the King went hunting, while his servants prepared the palace for the feast.

The night of the celebration, the palace was radiant. Everyone dressed in their finest and joined in the merriment. After dinner, the King quieted the crowd and called out to the Magician.

"Is it true that you can see the future?" he asked the old man.

"A little," answered the Magician.

"Then prove it," said the King. "Tell me the exact date of your death."

The Magician smiled, but didn't answer.

"What's wrong, Magician?" asked the King with a smirk. "Don't you know the answer?"

"It's not that," said the Magician. "It's just that I can't bring myself to tell you what I know."

"What do you mean by that?" bellowed the King. "I am your King, and I am ordering you to tell me!"

Suddenly, silence filled the royal hall.

After a moment, the Magician looked directly at the King and said:

"I can not tell Your Highness the exact date, but I do know the Magician of this kingdom will die the exact same day as his King."

At this, the guests stood silent. Gradually, the sound of murmurs started spreading through the hall.

The King stopped. He didn't believe in magic or superstitions, but he didn't dare risk his own life by killing the old man. His plan was ruined. Flustered, he fled the party.

As he raced through the palace hallways, he thought to himself, "What if something happened to the Magician on his way home tonight?"

The King turned around and quickly headed back, searching for the Magician. He found him still at the party.

"You must spend the night in the palace," the King told him, breathlessly.

"I, uh . . . I would like to talk to you about some royal matters that could use a Magician's insight!"

This was just an excuse, of course. The King wanted to keep an eye on the Magician so nothing would happen to him. As long as the Magician remained safe, the King would live on. The Magician bowed deeply and replied with a smile, "It will be a great honor, Your Majesty."

The King quickly ordered his servants to take the Magician to the finest guest room in the castle, make him comfortable, and carefully guard the door.

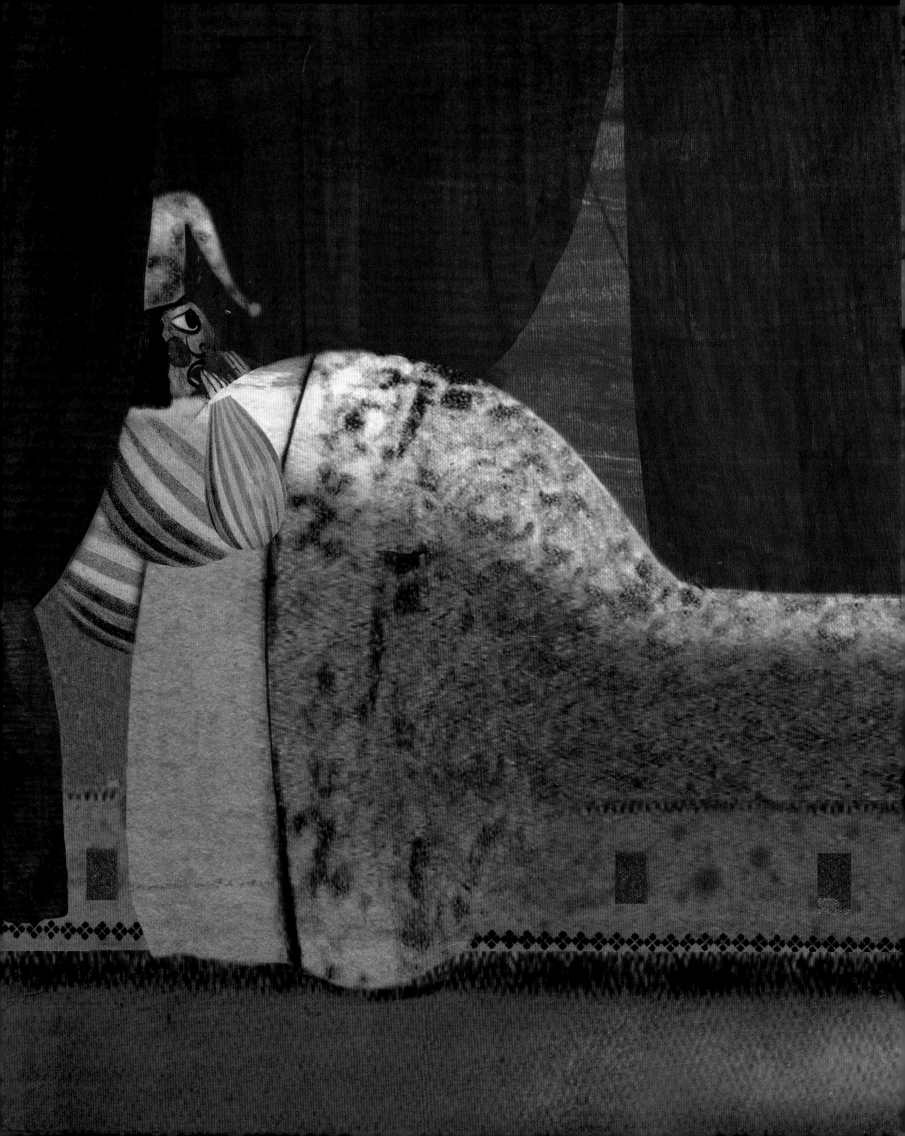

That night, the Magician slept comfortably on the softest mattress he had ever known, while the King, on his even softer mattress, couldn't sleep at all. He lay awake imagining all the dangers that could harm the Magician. What if his food was poisoned? What if he tripped and fell? What if a wild animal crept into his room? Anything that threatened the Magician was a threat to the King as well.

Early the next morning, the pale and restless King went to his guest's room.

He had never asked for advice before, but he needed an excuse to keep the Magician close. So he asked the old man his opinion about something related to running the kingdom.

Being a wise and just man, the Magician offered him good suggestions. The King thanked him and insisted he stay at the palace one more night, in case he wanted advice on another matter. The truth was, of course, that he was terrified about what could happen to the Magician, and therefore himself, if he left the palace.

Days, weeks, and months went by. Each morning, the King went to the Magician's room for advice, and each morning the King told the Magician to stay one more day to help him with yet another matter.

The Magician was amused by all the care and attention he received from his royal host, even if he got tired of waiting for the King's guards to inspect the garden for any danger every time he wanted to go out for fresh air.

More and more, the King came to value the guidance of the
Magician. Without even realizing it, the King started relying on the old
man's opinion for everything. That is how the King's once-feared enemy
became his most valued advisor.

The more time the King spent with the Magician, the more just, fair, and wise he became. The King turned into a respected leader, now truly beloved by all in his realm.

The day came when the King no longer went to see the Magician to keep him under his control. Instead he went because he wanted to learn from him, share his thoughts and decisions, and just be his friend. Many nights, while lying in bed, the King remembered how he had once considered this trusted friend his greatest enemy, and had planned to kill him. The memory filled his heart with shame, until he could bear the secret no more.

He gathered his courage and went to the Magician's room.

"My brother and friend, I have something to tell you that weighs heavily on my chest," confessed the King.

"Tell me," the Magician answered, "and rest your heart."

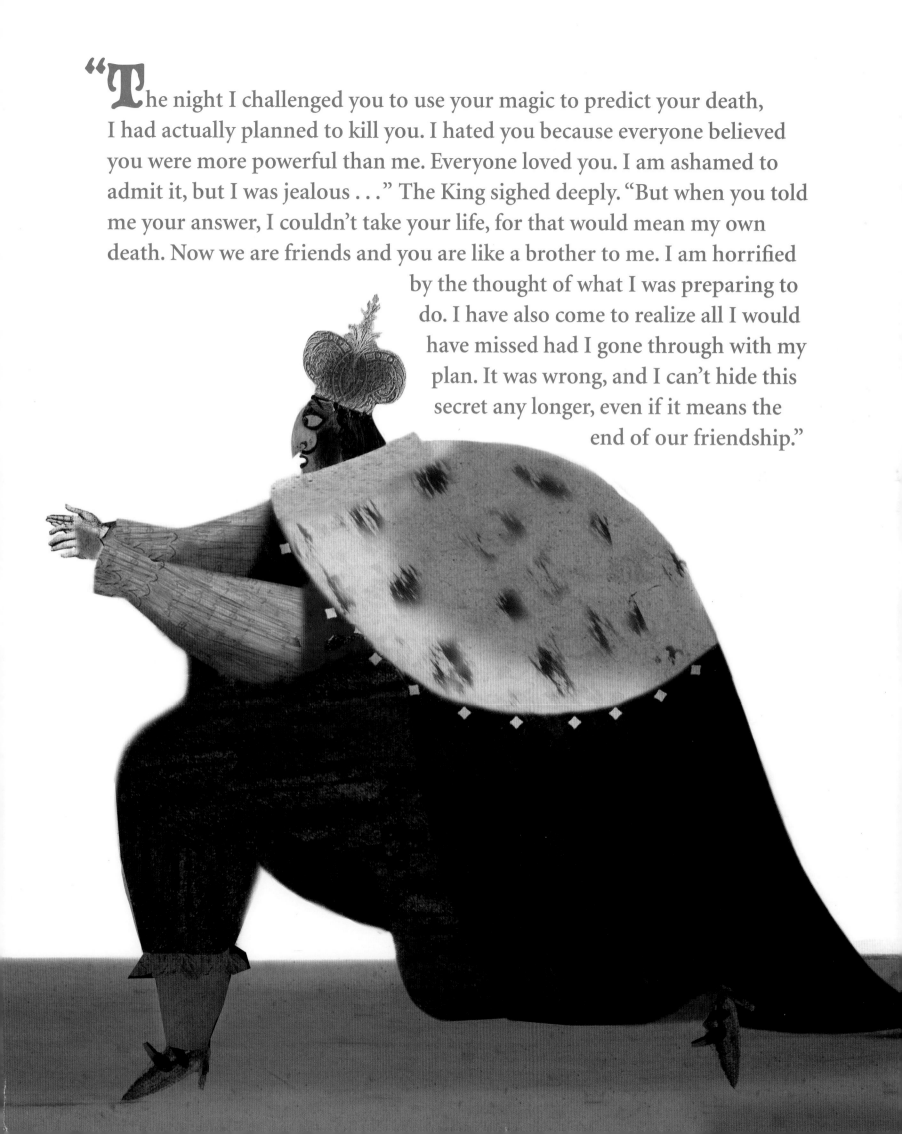

"The night I challenged you to use your magic to predict your death, I had actually planned to kill you. I hated you because everyone believed you were more powerful than me. Everyone loved you. I am ashamed to admit it, but I was jealous . . ." The King sighed deeply. "But when you told me your answer, I couldn't take your life, for that would mean my own death. Now we are friends and you are like a brother to me. I am horrified by the thought of what I was preparing to do. I have also come to realize all I would have missed had I gone through with my plan. It was wrong, and I can't hide this secret any longer, even if it means the end of our friendship."

The Magician looked at the King and said:
    "Let's go for a walk."
As they walked, the Magician said, "It has taken you a long time to tell me, but I am glad you did. That night, when you asked me to announce when I would die, I saw you place your hand on the hilt of your sword and your intentions became clear. I did not need to be a sorcerer or fortune-teller to see what was about to happen."

The Magician, with a twinkle in his eye, said, "As a reward for your honesty, I must tell you that I made up the prediction that our deaths would happen the same day. I did it to teach you a lesson, and I see that it has."

The Magician smiled and put his hand on the King's shoulder. "Your death, my dear friend, will come whenever it shall come, not one minute sooner. I am an old man, and my time will soon come to an end. I promise, you have no reason to think that your departure is tied to mine. It is our lives that have become entwined, not our deaths."

The King and his former enemy hugged one another, and celebrated their friendship with warmth and joy.

Many years passed. The kingdom grew strong, as did the love of the people for their King. He was now kinder and gentler because of all that he gained from his great friendship with the ragged old Magician.

Finally, one day, when he was very, very old, the Magician died. The King felt great sadness, but he was no longer afraid of dying that day or the next.

With his own hands, he dug the grave for his beloved friend in the gardens of the palace, right in front of his window.

Even though the Magician was no longer there, his face and his voice were always with the King. Every moment of the day, the King remembered the wise words and teachings of his greatest friend.

Whenever he needed to solve problems or make difficult decisions for the kingdom, the many memories of their friendship gave him strength and peace.

One day, ten years later, the King locked himself in his royal chamber and wrote a letter to his son, the future King.

That night, exactly ten years to the day after the Magician's death, the King died peacefully in his sleep. It was probably a coincidence, but everyone in the kingdom thought it fitting that the King chose to honor a friend, even in death.

Dear Son,

I know that my end is near and I want to give you my last piece of advice. One day, maybe tomorrow, maybe next month, or perhaps many years from now, you will come across something or someone who will arouse fear and jealousy in your soul. It might be a person or even something inside you. You will want to destroy that person or that feeling to drive away your fear. Don't do it! If you're able to open your heart or your home, you may discover that who or what you thought was your most feared enemy, is really your most powerful friend.

Your father who loves you,
The King, up to this day.